HAPPY BIRTHDAY!

to SHANNON♥

from WILL♥

HAPPY BIRTHDAY TO YOU!

By Dr. Seuss

RANDOM HOUSE · NEW YORK

TM & copyright © 1959, copyright renewed 1987, by Dr. Seuss Enterprises, L.P.

Published in the United States by Random House Children's Books,
a division of Random House LLC, a Penguin Random House Company, New York.
Originally published in a slightly different form in the United States
by Random House Children's Books, New York, in 1959.

Random House and the colophon are registered trademarks of Random House LLC.

Grateful acknowledgment is made to Dr. Seuss Enterprises, L.P.
for permission to reprint artwork and lyrics to
"Happy Birthday to Little Sally Spingel Spungel Sporn" by Dr. Seuss,
from *The Cat in the Hat Songbook,*
TM and copyright © 1967 by Dr. Seuss Enterprises, L.P. and Eugene Poddany.
Copyright renewed 1995 by Dr. Seuss Enterprises, L.P. and Oleg Poddany.

This special edition was printed for Target by Random House Children's Books,
a division of Random House LLC, New York.

Visit us on the Web!
Seussville.com
randomhouse.com/kids

Educators and librarians, for a variety of teaching tools, visit us at
RHTeachersLibrarians.com

ISBN 978-0-375-97381-9

Printed in the United States of America
10 9 8 7 6 5 4 3 2 1

For
my good friends,
The Children of San Diego County

I wish we could do what they do in Katroo.
They sure know how to say "Happy Birthday to You!"

In Katroo, every year, on the day you were born
They start the day right in the bright early morn
When the Birthday Honk-Honker hikes high up Mt. Zorn
And lets loose a big blast on the big Birthday Horn.
And the voice of the horn calls out loud as it plays:
"Wake Up! For today is your Day of all Days!"

Then, the moment the Horn's happy honk-honk is heard,
Comes a fluttering flap-flap! And then comes THE BIRD!

The Great Birthday Bird!
And, so far as I know,
Katroo is the only place Birthday Birds grow.
This bird has a brain. He's most beautifully brained
With the brainiest bird-brain that's ever been trained.
He was trained by the most splendid Club in this nation,
The Katroo Happy Birthday Asso-see-eye-ation.
And, whether your name is Pete, Polly or Paul,
When your birthday comes round, he's in charge of it all.

Whether your name is Nate, Nelly or Ned,
He knows your address, and he heads for your bed.
You hear a soft *swoosh* in the brightening sky.
You are not all awake. But you open one eye.
Then over the housetops and trees of Katroo,
You see that bird coming! To you. *Just to you!*

That Bird pops right in!

You are up on your feet!

You jump to the window! You meet and you greet

With the Secret Katroo Birthday Hi-Sign-and-Shake

That only good people with birthdays may make.

You do it just so. With each finger and toe.

Then the Bird says, "Come on! Brush your teeth and let's go!

It's your Day of all Days! It's the Best of the Best!

So don't waste a minute!

Hop to it!

Get dressed!"

And five minutes later, you're having a snack
On your way out of town on a Smorgasbord's back.
"Today," laughs the Bird, "eat whatever you want.
Today no one tells you you cawnt or you shawnt.
And, today, you don't have to be tidy or neat.
If you wish, you may eat with both hands and both feet.
So get in there and munch. Have a big munch-er-oo!
Today is your birthday! *Today you are you!*"

If we didn't have birthdays, you wouldn't be you.

If you'd never been born, well then what would you do?

If you'd never been born, well then what would you be?

You *might* be a fish! Or a toad in a tree!

You might be a doorknob! Or three baked potatoes!

You might be a bag full of hard green tomatoes.

Or worse than all that . . . Why, you might be a WASN'T!

A Wasn't has no fun at all. No, he doesn't.

A Wasn't just isn't. He just isn't present.

But you . . . You ARE YOU! And, now isn't that pleasant!

So we'll go to the top of the toppest blue space,
The Official Katroo Birthday Sounding-Off Place!
Come on! Open your mouth and sound off at the sky!
Shout loud at the top of your voice, "I AM I!
ME!
I am I!
And I may not know why
But I know that I like it.
Three cheers! I AM I!"

And now, on this Day of all Days in Katroo,
The Asso-see-eye-ation has built just for you
A railway with very particular boats
That are pulled through the air by Funicular Goats.
These goats never slip, never trip, never bungle.
They'll take us down fast to the Birthday Flower Jungle.
The best-sniffing flowers that anyone grows
We have grown to be sniffed by your own private nose.

They smell like licorice! And cheese!
Send forty Who-Bubs up the trees
To snip with snippers! Nip with nippers!
Clip and clop with clapping clippers.
Nip and snip with clipping cloppers!
Snip and snop with snipping snoppers!
All for you, the Who-Bubs clip!
Happy Birthday! Nop and nip!

Then pile the wondrous-smelling stacks
On fifty Hippo-Heimers' backs!
They'll take those flowers all home for you.
You can keep the Hippo-Heimers too.

    While this is done, I've got a hunch
    It's time to eat our Birthday Lunch . . .

For Birthday luncheons, as a rule,
We serve hot dogs, rolled on a spool.

  So stuff and stuff
  And stuff and stuff
  And stuff until you've had enough.

Now, of course, we're all mustard,
So, one of the rules
Is to wash it all off in the Mustard-Off Pools
Which are very fine warm-water mountaintop tubs
Which were built, just for this, by the Mustard-Off Clubs.

Then, out of the water! Sing loud while you dry!
Sing loud, "I am lucky!" Sing loud, "I am I!"

If you'd never been born, then you might be an ISN'T!
An Isn't has no fun at all. No he disn't.
He never has birthdays, and that isn't pleasant.
You have to be born, or you don't get a present.
A Present! *A-ha!*
Now what kind shall I give . . . ?
Why, the kind you'll remember
As long as you live!

Would you like a fine pet?
Well, that's just what you'll get.
I'll get you the fanciest pet ever yet!

As you see, we have here in the heart of our nation
The Official Katroo Birthday Pet Reservation.
From east of the East-est to west of the West-est
We've searched the whole world just to bring you the best-est.
They come in all sizes . . . small, medium, tall.
If you wish, I will find you the tallest of all!

To find who's the tallest,
We start with the smallest . . .

We start with the smallest. Then what do we do?
We line them all up. Back to back. Two by two.
Taller and taller. And, when we are through,
We finally will find one who's taller than who.

But you have to be smart and keep watching their feet.
Because sometimes they stand on their tiptoes and cheat.

And so, from the smaller, we stack 'em up taller
And taller. And taller. And taller and taller.
And now! Here's the one who is taller than all-er!
He's yours. He's all yours. He's the very top tallest.
I know you'll enjoy him. The tallest of all-est!

I'll have him shipped home to you, Birthday Express.
That costs quite a lot. But I couldn't care less.
Today is your birthday! Today You are You!
So what if it costs me a thousand or two.

Today is your birthday! You get what you wish.
You also might like a nice Time-Telling Fish.

So I'll send Diver Getz and I'll send Diver Gitz
Deep under the sea in their undersea kits.
In all the wide world there are no better pets
Than the Time-Telling Fish that Gitz gits and Getz gets.

But, speaking of time . . . Why, good gracious alive!
That Time-Telling Fish says it's quarter to five!
I had no idea it was getting so late!
We have to get going! We have a big date!

And so, as the sunset burns red in the west,
Comes the night of the Day-of-the-Best-of-the-Best!
The Night-of-All-Nights-of-All-Nights in Katroo!
So, according to rule, what we usually do
Is saddle up two Hooded Klopfers named Alice
And gallop like mad to the Birthday Pal-alace.
Your Big Birthday Party soon starts to begin
In the finest Pal-alace you've ever been in!

Now this Birthday Pal-alace, as soon you will see,
Has exactly nine thousand, four hundred and three
Rooms to play games in! Twelve halls for brass bands!
Not counting the fifty-three hamburger stands.
And besides all of that, there are sixty-five rooms
Just for keeping the Sweeping-Up-Afterwards-Brooms.
Because, after your party, as well you may guess,
It will take twenty days just to sweep up the mess.

First, we're greeted by Drummers who drum as they come.
And next come the Strummers who strum as they come.
And the Drummers who drum and Strummers who strum
Are followed by Zummers who come as they zum.
Just look at those Zummers! They're sort of like Plumbers.
They come along humming, with heads in their plumbing
And that makes the music that Zummers call zumming!

And all of this beautiful zumming and humming
And plumbing and strumming and drumming and coming . . .
All of it, all of it,
All is for you!

LOOK!

Dr. Derring's Singing Herrings!
Derring's Singing, Spelling Herrings!
See what Derring's Herrings do!
They sing and spell it! All for you!

And here comes your cake! Cooked by Snookers and Snookers,
The Official Katroo Happy Birthday Cake Cookers.
And Snookers and Snookers, I'm happy to say,
Are the only cake cookers who cook cakes today
Made of guaranteed, certified strictly Grade-A
Peppermint cucumber sausage-paste butter!
And the world's finest cake slicers, Dutter and Dutter
And Dutter and Dutter, with hatchets a-flutter,
High up on the poop deck, stand ready to cut her.

Today you are you! That is truer than true!
There is no one alive who is you-er than you!
Shout loud, "I am lucky to be what I am!
Thank goodness I'm not just a clam or a ham
Or a dusty old jar of sour gooseberry jam!
I am what I am! That's a great thing to be!
If I say so myself, HAPPY BIRTHDAY TO ME!"

Now, by Horseback and Bird-back and Hiffer-back, too,
Come your friends! All your friends! From all over Katroo!
And the Birthday Pal-alace heats up with hot friends
And your party goes on!
On and on
Till it ends.

When it ends,
You're much happier,
Richer and fatter.
And the Bird flies you home
On a very soft platter.

So that's
What the Birthday Bird
Does in Katroo.

And I wish
I could do
All these great things for *you!*

I am what I am!
   That's a great thing to be!
If I say so myself,
   HAPPY BIRTHDAY TO ME!

Today, _____,
                    (date)

is the day _____
                    (my name)

was born.

(paste photo here)

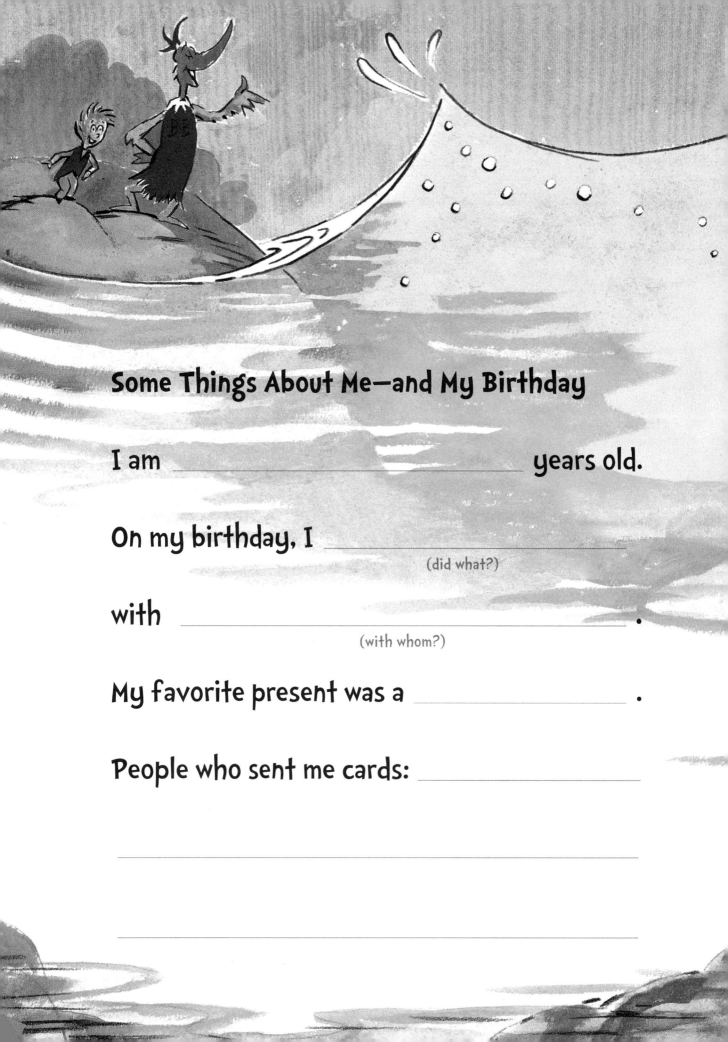

Some Things About Me—and My Birthday

I am _____ years old.

On my birthday, I _____
(did what?)

with _____ .
(with whom?)

My favorite present was a _____ .

People who sent me cards: _____

_____

_____

Today you are you! That is truer than true!
There is no one alive who is you-er than you!

(paste card or photo here)

(paste card or photo here)

"Today," laughs the Bird, "eat whatever you want.
Today no one tells you you cawnt or you shawnt."

On my birthday, we had a cake.

[ ] YES   [ ] NO

I ate:

☐ a small piece.

☐ a big piece.

☐ more than one piece.

☐ none at all. I don't eat cake!

I decorated this birthday cake:

Happy-Birthday Wishes from Friends and Family

I wish we could do what they do in Katroo.
They sure know how to say "Happy Birthday to You!"

A Birthday Poem
by Dr. Seuss

Happy Birthday to Little Sally Spingel Spungel Sporn

Happy birthday to little
Sally Spingel Spungel Sporn,
Who on this wondrous day
Was born.
And happy birthday also
To Fredric Futzenfell,
Who was born upon this
Wondrous day as well.
And happy birthday also
To Waldo Wilberforce.
Happy birthday likewise,
To Paul Revere's fine horse.
But most of all,
We sing to honor you,

SALLY

_____ ,
(honored name)

Born upon this great, great, great day too!

—from *The Cat in the Hat Songbook* by Dr. Seuss

So that's
What the Birthday Bird
Does in Katroo.
And I wish
I could do
All these great things for *you*!

Some things I wish for:

_____

_____

_____

_____

_____